This book belongs to

Donna

~ More Animal Stories ~

DICK KING-SMITH

~ More Animal Stories ~

Illustrated by Michael Terry

PUFFIN BOOKS

VIKING/PUFFIN

Published by the Penguin Group
Penguin Books Ltd, 27 Wrights Lane, London W8 5TZ, England
Penguin Putnam Inc., 375 Hudson Street, New York, New York 10014, USA
Penguin Books Australia Ltd, Ringwood, Victoria, Australia
Penguin Books Canada Ltd, 10 Alcorn Avenue, Toronto, Ontario, Canada M4V 3B2
Penguin Books (NZ) Ltd, Private Bag 102902, NSMC, Auckland, New Zealand

Penguin Books Ltd, Registered Offices: Harmondsworth, Middlesex, England

This collection first published 1999
1 3 5 7 9 10 8 6 4 2

'Poppet', 'The Spelling Bee' and 'The Septopus' copyright © Fox Busters Ltd, 1999

'Little Red Riding Pig', 'The Owl and the Pussy-cat', 'Goldipig and the Three Bears', 'Hogsel and Gruntel'
and 'The Princess and the Pig' were first published in 1991 by Victor Gollancz Ltd in
Dick King-Smith's Triffic Pig Book copyright © Fox Busters Ltd, 1991

'Dumpling' was first published in 1986 by Hamish Hamilton Ltd copyright © Dick King-Smith, 1986

'Dinosaur School' (under the title 'Use Your Brains') and 'Norty Boy' were first published in 1993
by Viking in *A Narrow Squeak and Other Animal Stories* copyright © Fox Busters Ltd, 1993

'The Ugly Duckling' was first published in 1992 by Victor Gollancz Ltd in *The Topsy-Turvy Storybook*
copyright © Fox Busters Ltd, 1992

'The Great Sloth Race' copyright © Fox Busters Ltd, 1994

'Blessu' was first published in 1990 by Hamish Hamilton Ltd copyright © Fox Busters Ltd, 1990

'Zap!' copyright © Dick King-Smith, 1987

Illustrations copyright © Michael Terry, 1999

The moral right of the author and illustrator has been asserted

Filmset in 16pt Bembo

Printed at Oriental Press, Dubai, U.A.E

British Library Cataloguing in Publication Data
A CIP catalogue record for this book is available from the British Library

ISBN 0–670–88218–6

Contents

Poppet

When Poppet was born, he had absolutely no idea what sort of animal he was.

He looked around, and saw that he was surrounded by a forest of legs. Huge legs they were, thick and tall and greyish in colour, with huge feet on the end of them.

Poppet looked up, and saw, on top of all those legs, huge bodies with huge heads and huge ears and amazingly long, long noses.

He was in fact looking up at his mother, and a number of his aunties who had all come along to inspect this new baby.

'Oh!' said one auntie. 'Isn't he a poppet!'

The baby's mother looked extremely pleased.

'What are you going to call him?' said another auntie.

The baby's mother, whose own name was Ooma, said, 'I don't know, I haven't had time to think,' and then she thought for a bit, and then she said, 'But now I do know. I'll call him Poppet.' And she put the tip of her trunk against one of the baby's ears and whispered, 'Hello, baby. I'm your mum, and your name is Poppet.'

Poppet looked up at Ooma and the other huge animals and said, 'Please, what sort of animals are you?'

'Elephants,' said Ooma. 'We are African elephants.'

'Oh,' said Poppet. 'But you said you were my mum.'

'Yes.'

'So does that make me an African elephant?'

'Yes.'

Poppet looked puzzled. There must be some mistake, he thought. 'You're enormous,' he said, 'and I'm very small. We can't be the same sort of animal.'

'Oh yes we are,' said Ooma. 'It's just that you're a baby elephant.'

2

'But you'll grow,' said one of the aunties.

'And grow,' said another.

'And grow.'

'And grow.'

'And grow,' said all the others.

'Until you're as big as we are,' said Ooma. 'You might even be bigger one day.'

'Tomorrow?' said Poppet.

At this, the aunties all laughed quietly, making snuffly noises in their trunks, before moving slowly and heavily away, leaving mother and baby alone together.

'No, not tomorrow, Poppet,' said Ooma gently. 'Elephants take a long, long time to grow to full size. But you'll get there one day. There's nothing to stop you, for we are too big and our skins are too thick for any other creature in Africa to hurt us. Except two.'

'What are they, Mum?' asked Poppet.

'One,' said Ooma, 'is a monkey-like thing called a man. Men kill elephants.'

'Why?'

'For their tusks.'

'What are tusks?'

'Great big long teeth that elephants have. Like these two of mine.'

'I haven't got any.'

'You will. But you should be all right, because we live in a special place called a reserve, where elephants are protected.'

'Oh,' said Poppet. 'But you said there were *two* creatures that could hurt us. What's the other one, besides a man?'

'A mouse,' said Ooma.

'Oh,' said Poppet. 'Are they even bigger and stronger than us, these mouses?'

'Mice,' said Ooma, 'are very small and, what's more, mice live in holes, and that's the trouble.'

She stretched out her long, long trunk till the tip of it was right in front of Poppet's face.

'What do you see, Poppet?' she said.

'A hole,' said Poppet.

Then Ooma, speaking slowly and solemnly, repeated to her newborn child the old elephant-wives' tale that her mother had told her when she was a baby, a tale in which she had always believed.

'Poppet, my son,' she said. 'First, never have anything to do with mice. Second, if you should be unfortunate enough to meet one, keep your trunk curled up out of the way. Never, never put the tip of it anywhere near a mouse, otherwise the most dreadful thing imaginable will happen to you.'

their great cushioned feet, only to see her son with his trunk outstretched, the tip of it only centimetres from a mouse!

She let out a furious trumpet, and Momo vanished from sight.

'What did I tell you?' screamed Ooma. 'Keep away from mice, d'you hear me? Get out of my way now and I'll squash this one flat.'

'Oh, don't, Mum!' cried Poppet. 'He's my friend!'

'Your friend!' snorted Ooma. 'You're not just a bad child, you're a mad child.' And she went stamping about in the grass till she'd flattened a big patch of it.

'That should have fixed the horrid creature,' she said, and she moved away to rejoin the herd, grumbling to herself.

Poppet stood sadly beside the trampled patch.

'Alas, poor mouse!' he said. 'It's all my fault that he's dead.'

'No he isn't,' said a voice, and

out of the grass poked a little brown head, whiskers twitching.

'Momo!' cried Poppet. 'You're not hurt?'

'Got a bit of a headache.'

'How on earth did you survive?'

'Under earth. Went down a hole, sharpish,' said the mouse. 'But not before I heard what you said. Which was nice of you, Poppet. You are my friend too.'

Meanwhile, Ooma was telling the aunties about her naughty child.

'One of the first things I told him,' she said, 'was to keep away from mice. We all know that every mouse is just waiting for a chance to run up the inside of our trunks.'

'We do,' said the aunties.

'And no doubt you all gave your kids the same warning.'

'We did,' said the aunties.

'And what have I just found? Only my boy with the tip of his trunk right beside a mouse, that's all. I told him off, I can tell you. No doubt you'd have done the same?'

'We would,' said the aunties.

'Children!' said Ooma. 'They just don't listen.'

'Grown-ups!' said Poppet to Momo at about the same time. 'They don't treat children fairly, grown-ups don't. I could have explained to Mum if she'd let me. I could have told her, "You're wrong. Mice don't run up elephants' trunks. I know. My friend told me." But no, I never got the chance. She just yelled at me.'

'I heard it,' said Momo.

'Let's just hope we're more understanding when we're grown-ups,' said Poppet.

17

'Actually,' said Momo, 'I'm a grown-up already.'

'Oh, sorry! I didn't realize. You're so . . . um . . .'

'Small?'

'Well, yes.'

'Tell you what, Poppet,' said the mouse. 'Do you agree that it would be a good thing if elephants stopped being frightened of mice?'

'Yes, I do.'

'And do you agree that it would be a good thing if elephants stopped trying to squash mice?'

'Oh yes, I do.'

'Right then. This is my plan. Listen carefully.'

And so it was that later that day, when the herd had been down to the river to bathe and the elephants were all standing in the shade, resting, Poppet said to Ooma, 'Mum, will you promise not to yell at me if I tell you something?'

'Of course I won't,' said Ooma, who was already rather ashamed of losing her temper with her little one.

'Of course you won't promise?'

'No. Of course I won't yell at you.'

'All right then,' said Poppet. 'It's this. Mice do not run up inside elephants' trunks. They never have and they never will.'

Ooma snorted.

'Come and listen to this,' she called to the aunties, and when they had all gathered round, she made Poppet repeat his words.

'Silly boy,' said one auntie, and, 'Stupid child,' said another, and a third said, 'You had a narrow escape this morning. You might not be so lucky another time.'

'Wait here, please,' said Poppet, and he disappeared into

some bushes. When he emerged again, Ooma and the aunties could see that he was holding something in the tip of his trunk, something furry and brown, with large tulip-shaped ears, beady black eyes and a longish hairless tail – a mouse!

How horrified they all were! They formed a circle around Poppet, their trunks held high out of the reach of the dreaded creature that he carried, and they shifted anxiously from foot to foot, fanning their great ears.

Poppet put the mouse carefully down upon the ground.

'This is Momo,' he said to Ooma and the aunties. 'My friend, like I told you, Mum. I know I am only a child, but Momo is a grown-up, even though you may think he's not grown very far. However, he has a grown-up brain, I can tell you, and he wishes to address you all, if you will be kind enough to listen to him.'

So astonished were the elephants, first to see Poppet carrying the mouse, and then to hear him make such a speech, that they stopped fidgeting and stood, silent, except for the rumbling of their tummies, which they couldn't help.

Momo sat up on his hunkers.

'Ladies,' he said. 'It is a great privilege to be allowed to speak to you, and,' he turned to face Ooma, 'especially you, madam, the mother of a truly remarkable child.'

Elephants can't blush, but if Ooma could have done, she would have done.

'Poppet,' the mouse went on, 'is a name that all elephants will remember for all time, since it is he – with a little help from myself – who has been the first of his kind to discover that mice do *not*, never have, and never will run up the inside of elephants' trunks. I call upon him now to conclude this historic day by offering to all of you the proof of what I have just said. So that none of you here, indeed none of your kind throughout the length and breadth of Africa, needs ever again worry about meeting a mouse, trunk to face. Now Poppet, say your piece.'

'Mum,' said Poppet. 'Do you love me?'

'Oh yes, Poppet,' said Ooma.

'Would you do anything for me?'

'Oh yes.'

'Then uncurl your trunk and stretch out the tip of it to Momo.'

'Oh no, Poppet! I couldn't!'

'Courage, madam,' said Momo, while all the aunties cried, 'Go on, Ooma!' safe in the knowledge that they didn't have to do it.

'It'll be all right, Mum,' said Poppet. 'Honest.'

So very slowly, with her eyes tight shut, Ooma uncoiled her trunk and laid the tip of it on the ground, right beside the mouse. Momo peered up it, careful (remembering Poppet's sneeze) not to touch it with his whiskers.

'Yuck!' he said softly.

Then he said to Ooma, 'Thank you, madam. I appreciate

your confidence and your courage, and I am filled with admiration for the undoubted beauty, strength and dexterity of your magnificent nasal appendage. I hope, however, that you will forgive me if I say that nothing in this world could ever persuade me to creep up your trunk.'

'I had a job to keep a straight face,' said Momo when the herd had moved away, shaking their great heads in wonder at what they had just seen and heard. Ooma especially seemed quite overcome by what had happened, and when Poppet said to her, 'Mum, can I stay and play with Momo?' she answered, 'Yes, of course, dear,' as though hypnotized.

When they were alone, Poppet said, 'What shall we play? Can you think of a game?'

'Yes,' said Momo. 'Put down your trunk and I'll run up it.'

'Oh no!' cried Poppet. 'You mean it's true after all, what Mum told me? And I thought you were my friend!'

'I am,' said Momo. 'Don't get your trunk in a twist. I just want to run up the *outside*.'

Little Red Riding Pig

Little Red Riding Pig set out one day to visit her grandmother. She was called Little Red Riding Pig because she was small, of a ginger colour, and always rode about on her mountain bike.

Cycling through a forest glade, she met a wolf.

'Hold it right there, baby,' said the wolf.

Little Red Riding Pig held it.

'Where you headin'?' said the wolf.

'To visit my grandmother,' replied Little Red Riding Pig.

The wolf thought quickly. Not a lot of meat on this

piglet, he said to himself, but the granny – now she might
make a square meal.

'Your granny kinda fat?' he asked in a casual way.

'Oh yes!' said Little Red Riding Pig. 'She's very fat.'

'Sure like to meet her,' said the wolf. 'She live around here
some place?'

'Oh yes!' said Little Red Riding Pig, and she told the
wolf how to get to her grandmother's house, and away he
went.

When he arrived, he knocked on the door and a voice
called, 'Come in, my dear,' so he did.

There, lying in bed, was the fattest pig the wolf had ever
seen.

'Goodness me!' said the pig. 'I thought you were my little
granddaughter.'

''Fraid not, ma'am,' said the wolf.

'But I see now,' said Little Red Riding Pig's grandmother,
'that you are in fact a handsome stranger. What big ears you
have!'

All the better to hear you with, thought the wolf, but he
kept his mouth shut.

'And what big eyes you have!'

All the better to see you with, thought the wolf, but he said nothing, merely opening his jaws in a kind of silent laugh.

'And what big teeth you have!' said the fat pig, and before the wolf could think about that, she went on, 'Which reminds me, I have the toothache. I should be so grateful if you could look and see which tooth is causing the trouble.'

'Why, sure, ma'am,' said the wolf, and he approached the bed, dribbling slightly at the thought of the feast in store.

The fat pig opened her mouth wide, and the wolf bent his head to look into it.

Not long afterwards Little Red Riding Pig came pedalling up on her mountain bike. Usually, when she knocked on the door, her grandmother would call, 'Come in, my dear,' but now all she heard was a grunt.

She opened the door.

Her grandmother looked even fatter than usual. And there was something else odd about her.

'Why, Granny,' cried Little Red Riding Pig in amazement, 'you have grown a long grey beard!'

But it was only the wolf's tail, still sticking out of her grandmother's mouth.

The Owl and the Pussy-cat

You all know that the Owl and the Pussy-cat went to

sea in a beautiful pea-green boat. But do you remember

the Piggy-wig they met in a wood with a ring

at the end of his nose? And do you ever wonder

what he did with the shilling that they gave him?

Well, read on . . .

S aid the Piggy, 'I will.'

'At last,' said the Piggy-wig, 'I can rootle!'

Rootling in the ground with their strong snouts

is something all pigs love doing, but they cannot rootle if they have rings in their noses.

'At last,' said the Piggy-wig again, 'I am rid of that horrid ring. And what's more, that Owl and that Pussy-cat actually paid me for it! A whole shilling! Though I do not know what on earth to do with it. But talking of earth gives me an idea,' and he dug a little hole with his snout and buried the shilling in a safe place, under the Bong-tree. Then off he went all around the wood, rootling and rootling to his heart's content.

He had turned up all sorts of nice things – bulbs and roots and beetles – when suddenly his snout struck upon something hard. It was a large spoon, whose handle had been bent at right angles to its bowl by the force of the pig's rootling.

At that moment the turkey who lives on the hill came strutting by.

'That spoon won't be much use to you at the wedding-feast,' he said.

'I haven't been asked,' said the pig.

'Pity,' said the turkey. 'They're having mince. And slices of quince.'

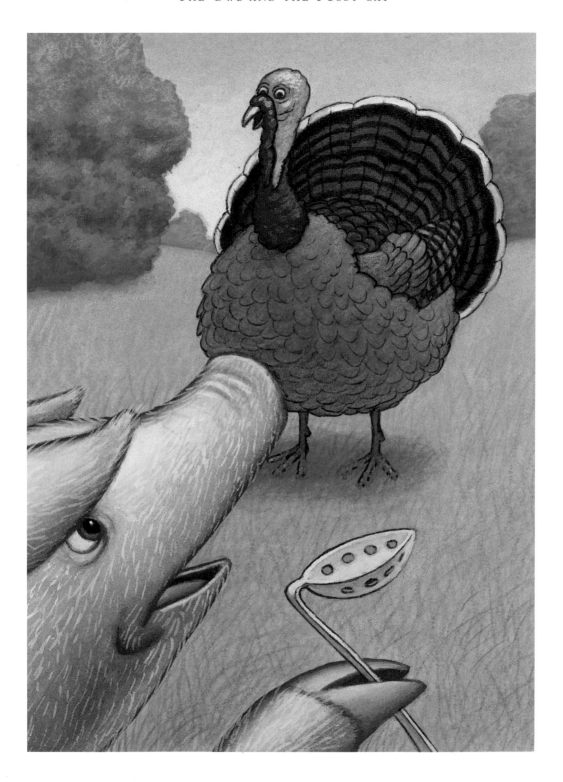

The pig licked his lips.

'I could get you an invite,' said the turkey.

'Could you?' said the pig eagerly.

'At a price.'

'How much?'

'One shilling.'

'Done!' said the pig, and he rushed back to the Bong-tree and dug up his shilling and gave it to the turkey.

Next day the Owl and the Pussy-cat were married by the turkey who lives on the hill. All the invited guests (including the pig) were there, and all had brought wedding presents (except the pig).

'What can I give them?' he whispered anxiously to the turkey, who sniggered and replied, 'Give 'em that old spoon.'

Quickly, for he did not want to miss the wedding-feast, the pig ran back to the wood and found the spoon.

When he returned with it, he could see that something was wrong. The Pussy-cat was in tears, the Owl was trying to comfort her, and the guests were tut-tutting and dear-dearing among themselves.

'All ruined!' cried the Pussy-cat. 'All wasted!'

'O lovely Pussy!' said the Owl. 'Whatever's the matter?'

'Mince!' cried the Pussy-cat. 'And slices of quince! There's only one possible way to eat them and that we cannot do!'

At this moment the Piggy-wig pushed his way through the crowd of guests, and dropped before the unhappy couple the large spoon with the right-angled handle.

'Hope you'll be very happy,' he said gruffly.

'O Piggy-wig!' cried the Pussy-cat, drying her tears.

'Now we most certainly shall be! Your wedding present is the one thing that we needed, the one thing without which it is not possible to dine on mince, and slices of quince!'

'O Pussy my love!' said the Owl, looking in puzzlement at the Piggy-wig's present. 'What is it?'

'You elegant fowl!' laughed the Pussy-cat joyfully. 'It's a runcible spoon!'

Dumpling

'Oh, how I long to be long!' said Dumpling.

'Who do you want to belong to?' asked one of her brothers.

'No, I don't mean to *belong*,' said Dumpling. 'I mean, BE LONG!'

When the three dachshund puppies had been born, they had looked much like pups of any other breed.

Then, as they became older, the two brothers began to grow long, as dachshunds do. Their noses moved further and further away from their tail-tips.

35

But the third puppy stayed short and stumpy.

'How long you are getting,' said the lady who owned them all to the two brothers.

She called one of them Joker because he was always playing silly games, and the other one Thinker, because he liked to sit and think deeply.

Then she looked at their sister and shook her head.

'You are nice and healthy,' she said. 'Your eyes are bright and your coat is shining and you're good and plump. But dachshunds are supposed to have long bodies, you know. And you haven't. You're just a little dumpling.'

Dumpling asked her mother about the problem.

'Will I ever grow really long like Joker and Thinker?' she asked.

Her mother looked at her plump daughter and sighed.

'Time will tell,' she said.

Dumpling asked her brother, Joker.

'Joker,' she said. 'How can I grow longer?'

'That's easy, Dumpy,' said Joker. 'I'll hold your nose and Thinker will hold your tail and we'll stretch you.'

'Don't be silly, Joker,' said Thinker.

Thinker was a serious puppy. He did not like to play

jokes. 'It would hurt Dumpy if we did that.'

'Well then, what shall I do, Thinker?' asked Dumpling.

Thinker thought deeply. Then he said, 'Try going for long walks. And it helps if you take very long steps.'

So Dumpling set off the next morning. All the dachshunds were out in the garden. The puppies' mother was snoozing in the sunshine.

Joker was playing a silly game pretending that a stick was a snake.

Thinker was sitting and thinking deeply.

Dumpling slipped away through a hole in the hedge.

Next to the garden was a wood, and she set off between the trees on her very short legs. She stepped out boldly, trying hard to imagine herself growing a tiny bit longer with each step. Suddenly she bumped into a large black cat which was sitting under a yew tree.

'Oh, I beg your

pardon!' said Dumpling.

'Granted,' said the cat. 'Where are you going?'

'Oh, nowhere special. I'm just taking a long walk. You see, I'm trying to grow longer,' and she went on to explain about dachshunds and how they should look.

'Everyone calls me Dumpling,' she said sadly. 'I wish I could be long.'

'Granted,' said the black cat again.

'What do you mean?' she said. 'Can you make me long?'

'Easy as winking,' said the cat, winking. 'I'm a witch's cat. I'll cast a spell on you. How long do you want to be?'

'Oh very, very long!' cried Dumpling excitedly. 'The longest dachshund ever!'

The black cat stared at her with his green eyes, and then he shut them and began to chant:

> 'Abra-cat-abra,
>
> Hark to my song,
>
> It will make you
>
> Very long.'

The sound of the cat's voice died away and the wood was suddenly very still.

39

Then the cat gave himself a shake and opened his eyes.

'Remember,' he said, 'you asked for it.'

'Oh, thank you, thank you!' said Dumpling. 'I feel longer already. Will I see you again?'

'I shouldn't wonder,' said the cat.

Dumpling set off back towards the garden. The feeling of growing longer was lovely. She wagged her tail madly, and each wag seemed a little further away than the last.

She thought how surprised Joker and Thinker would be. She would be much longer than them.

'Dumpling, indeed!' she said. 'I will have to have a new name now, a very long one to match my new body.'

But then she began to find walking difficult. Her front feet knew where they were going, but her back feet acted very oddly. They seemed to be a long way behind her.

They kept tripping over things, and dropping into rabbit-holes.

They kept getting stuck among the bushes. She couldn't see her tail, so she went round a big tree to look for it and met it on the other side.

By now, she was wriggling on her tummy like a snake.

'Help!' yapped Dumpling at the top of her voice. 'Cat, come back, please!'

'Granted,' said the witch's cat, appearing suddenly beside her. 'What's the trouble now?'

'Oh please,' cried Dumpling, 'undo your spell!'

'Some people are never satisfied,' said the cat. Once more he stared at her with his green eyes.

Then he shut them and began to chant:

       'Abra-cat-abra,

       Hear my song,

       It will make you

       Short not long.'

Dumpling never forgot how wonderful it felt as her back feet came towards her front ones, and her tummy rose from the ground.

She hurried homewards, and squeezed her nice, comfortable, short, stumpy body through the hole in the hedge.

Joker and Thinker came galloping across the grass towards her.

How clumsy they look, she thought, with those silly long bodies.

'Where have you been, Dumpy?' shouted Joker.

'Did the exercise make you longer?' asked Thinker.

'No,' said Dumpling. 'But as a matter of fact, I'm quite happy as I am now. And that's about the long and the short of it!'

Goldipig and the Three Bears

Goldipig was a very inquisitive little swine, always poking her snout into other people's business.

Rooting about in the forest one day, she came upon a house among the trees. 'I wonder who lives there?' said Goldipig, and when she had called 'Hello!' and no one had answered, she pushed open the door and went in.

The first thing she saw was a table with three chairs around it, one big, one ordinary-sized, one little, and on the table in front of each chair was a bowl of porridge, one big, one ordinary-sized, one little.

Goldipig scoffed the lot.

Then, nosy as ever, she trotted upstairs. There in a bedroom were three beds, one big, one ordinary-sized, one little.

'I'll have a nap,' said Goldipig, feeling rather full.

She tried each bed in turn. The first was too little, the second too ordinary, but the third, the big bed, was just right, so Goldipig snuggled down and went to sleep.

Shortly afterwards the owners of the house returned. They had been taking a walk to work up an appetite for breakfast. They were in fact three bears, one big, one ordinary-sized, one little.

'Who's been sitting on our chairs?' said the little bear.

'And where's our porridge gone?' said the ordinary-sized bear.

'And who,' said the big bear, listening carefully, 'is that snoring upstairs?'

Very quietly the three bears climbed to the bedroom and looked in and saw Goldipig.

'She's messed up all our beds,' said the little bear.

'After eating all our porridge,' said the ordinary-sized bear.

'And so,' said the big bear, 'we'll jolly well eat her.'

At that, Goldipig let out an enormous squeal, dashed past the bears and rushed downstairs and away. So you can see the three of them got neither porridge nor ham for their breakfast!

The
Spelling
Bee

For weeks Noah's Ark had been sailing about on the
great waters of the Flood, and the animals were
getting very bored.

Noah noticed this.

'They haven't got enough to do,' he said to Mrs Noah.
'They need to use their brains. We'll have a competition.'

'What sort of competition?' said Mrs Noah.

Noah thought for a bit, and then he said, 'A spelling
competition.'

'We're going to have a spelling competition,' he told all

the animals, 'to see who is the cleverest among you. Who would like to take part?'

One of the two elephants pushed forward.

'I am the biggest animal in the Ark,' it said, 'so it stands to reason that I must be the cleverest. What do you want me to spell?'

'Your name,' said Noah.

'That's easy,' said the elephant. 'E...L...L...'

'Stop!' said Noah. 'I'm afraid you're spelling that wrong. Next, please.'

'I am the tallest animal in the Ark,' said one of the two giraffes, 'so it stands to reason that I must be the cleverest. What do you want me to spell?'

'Your name,' said Noah.

'That's easy,' said the giraffe. 'J...I...R...'

'Hold it!' said Noah. 'I'm afraid you're spelling that wrong. Next, please.'

'I have the thickest skin of any of the animals in the Ark,' said one of the two rhinoceroses, 'so it stands to reason that I must be the cleverest. What do you want me to spell?'

'Your name,' said Noah again.

'That's easy,' said the rhinoceros. 'R...I...N...'

'Hang on!' said Noah. 'I'm afraid you're spelling that wrong. Next please.'

Then one of the two monkeys scampered up.

'I must be the cleverest,' it said. 'The others didn't know what you wanted them to spell, but I do. You want me to spell my name.'

'Go on then,' said Noah.

'It couldn't be simpler,' said the monkey. 'M...U...N...'

'Whoa!' said Noah. 'You're wrong too. In fact it's beginning to look as though there isn't one animal that can spell its name correctly. Would anyone else like to have a try?'

At that moment one of the two bees on board the Ark came flying along and chanced to land on Noah's hand.

'Aha!' said Noah. 'Here's someone else wanting to take part in our competition.'

52

'Who, me?' said the bee.

'Yes, you,' said Noah.

'But I'm no good at spelling,' said the bee.

'Oh, go on!' said Noah. 'Have a try. Tell us how you spell your name.'

'My name?' said the bee.

'Yes.'

'Bee?' said the bee.

'Yes!' cried Noah. 'That's right. B. Go on.'

The bee sat silent, so Noah gave it a little pinch to encourage it. 'Eee!' cried the bee.

'Yes,' said Noah. 'E. Keep going.' And he gave it another little pinch.

'Eee!' cried the bee again.

'That's it!' shouted Noah. 'You've done it. B...E...E. You and you alone have spelled your name correctly. So you must be the cleverest animal in the Ark.'

'Who, me?' said the bee.

'Yes, you,' said Noah. 'So you can buzz off now.'

And then everybody (except the elephant and the giraffe and the rhinoceros and the monkey) gave three hearty cheers for the clever little bee.

'What?' said Araminta.

'He said to me, "I'm twice as clever as you are."'

'Is he?' said Herb.

'Of course he isn't,' said Araminta hastily. 'He was just being silly and childish. I'm sure he won't be any trouble in the future.'

'Not in my playschool he won't,' said the stegosaurus and then, oddly, she used the very words that Araminta had used earlier.

'One of these days,' she said, 'he'll get into real trouble.' And off she waddled, flapping her back plates angrily.

And one of those days, Basil did.

Being expelled from playschool hadn't worried him at all. What do I want with other dinosaurs? he thought. I'm far superior to them, with my two brains, one to work my neck and my front legs, one to work my back legs and my tail. Brontosauruses are twice as clever as other dinosaurs and I'm twice as clever as any other brontosaurus.

You couldn't say that Basil was big-headed, for that was almost the smallest part of him, but you could certainly say that he was boastful, conceited and arrogant.

'That boy!' said Araminta to Herb. 'He's boastful, conceited and arrogant. He must get it from your side of the family, swaggering about and picking fights all the time. What does he think he is? A *Tyrannosaurus rex*?'

'What do you think you are?' Basil was saying at that very moment. He had come out of the lake where the family spent almost all their time, and set off for a walk.

He was ambling along, thinking what a fine fellow he was, when suddenly he saw a strange, smallish dinosaur standing in his path.

It was not like any dinosaur he had ever seen before. It stood upright on its hind legs, which were much bigger than its little forelegs, and it had a large head with large jaws and a great many teeth. But compared to Basil, who already weighed a couple of tonnes, it looked quite small, and he advanced upon it, saying in a rude tone, 'What do you think you are?'

'I'm a *Tyrannosaurus rex*,' said the stranger.

'Never heard of you,' said Basil.

'Lucky you.'

'Why? What's so wonderful about you? You can't even walk on four feet like a decent dinosaur and you've only got one brain. You'll be telling me next that you don't eat waterweed like we do.'

'We don't,' said the other. 'We only eat meat.'

'What sort of meat?'

'Brontosaurus, mostly.'

'Let's get this straight,' said Basil. 'Are you seriously telling me that you kill brontosauruses and eat them?'

'Yes.'

'Don't make me laugh,' said Basil. 'I'm four times as big as you.'

'Yes,' said the youngster, 'but my dad's four times as big as you. Oh, look, what a bit of luck, here he comes!'

Basil looked up to see a terrifying sight.

Marching towards him on its huge hind legs was a towering, full-grown *Tyrannosaurus rex* with a mouthful of long razor-sharp teeth. All of a sudden Basil had two brainwaves.

Time I went, he thought. Sharpish. And as one brain sent a message rippling along to the other, he turned tail and made for the safety of the lake as fast as his legs could carry him.

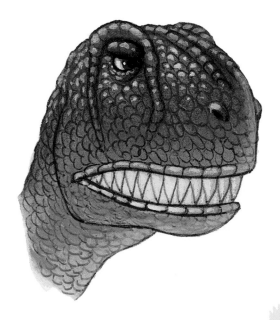

This was not very fast, as Basil's big body made him slow and clumsy on land. If the tyrannosaurus had been really hungry, he would have caught Basil without any trouble.

As it was, Basil reached the shore of the lake just in time and splashed frantically out to deeper water, where his parents, their long necks outstretched, were browsing on the weedy bottom.

Araminta was the first to look up.

'Hello, darling,' she said. 'Where have you been? Whatever's the matter? You're all of a doodah.'

'Oh, Mummy, Mummy!' panted Basil. 'It was awful! I went for a walk and I was nearly eaten by a *Tyrannosaurus rex*!'

Herb raised his head in time to hear this.

'That'll teach you,' he said.

'Teach me what, Dad?'

'Not to be so cocky,' said Araminta. 'Ever since I told you that secret you've been unbearable, Basil. I hope this will be a lesson to you.'

'Oh, it will, Mummy, it will!' cried Basil. 'I won't ever shoot my mouth off again.'

'And don't go for walks,' said his mother, 'but keep close to the lake, where you'll be safe from the tyrannosaurus.'

'In case he rex you,' said Herb, and plunged his head under water again, while strings of bubbles rose as he laughed at his own joke.

'And if you want to grow up to be as big as your father,' said Araminta, 'there's one thing you must always remember to do.'

'What's that, Mummy?' said Basil.

'Use your brains.'

The Ugly Duckling

An ordinary farmyard duck once hatched out a brood of ordinary ducklings. But when they were all free of their eggshells and scuttering about as newborn ducklings do, there was still one egg left in the nest.

It was a much bigger egg than the others had been, and the duck continued doggedly to sit upon it, hoping that it, too, would hatch. Which, some days later, it did.

Soon the duck could see that this last child was unlike his brothers and sisters. He was larger, he was greyish where

they were yellow, and his legs and feet were bigger and his neck much longer than theirs.

The duck thought him quite beautiful, and, proud mother that she was, she constantly told him so.

'You, my son,' she said, day in, day out, 'are beautiful. Your brothers and sisters are healthy normal ordinary ducklings, but you alone are beautiful,' and she constantly showed him off to the other birds in the farmyard, the hens and the geese and the turkeys.

'Look at him,' the old duck said to them, day in, day out. 'Is he not the most beautiful duckling you ever set eyes on?'

Not surprisingly, after all this constant flattery, the beautiful duckling grew up to be extremely big-headed.

He would stand by the duck pond and look at his reflection and say to himself, 'Observe my noble body and my powerful wings and my great webbed feet and my long and elegant neck. What a truly beautiful duckling I am!'

And at last, to cap it all, his plumage which had been grey turned to a brilliant snowy whiteness.

One day the beautiful duckling left the duck pond and made his way to a nearby lake. Here he stood by the water's edge and looked once more at his reflection.

'Without doubt,' he said, 'I must be the most beautiful duckling in the world. No other could compare with me.'

Then he looked up and saw a whole flock of great white birds swimming on the surface of the lake, birds that looked just like him, birds that certainly could compare with him.

'Even so, they cannot be as beautiful as I,' he said to himself, and he swam proudly out to meet them.

At the sight of this stranger approaching the swans banded together, arching their wings and hissing angrily.

'Who are you?' they cried, and the reply came, 'Make

way! I am the beautiful duckling.'

'Duckling!' said one of the swans to the rest, and, 'He's mad!' said another. 'And he's a big-head!' said a third, and then a host of voices said, 'Let's duck the duckling!'

And with that all the swans set upon the newcomer.

They buffeted him with their wings, and pecked at him, and pulled out his tail feathers, and finally they ducked his head under water.

Somehow, he struggled back to the duck pond, and saw the old duck who had hatched him so long ago but now did not recognize the battered, muddied bird, his neck limp, his wings trailing, his plumage all in dirty disarray.

'Who on earth are you?' she said.

'The beautiful duckling!' he gasped.

'A duckling you may be,' said the old duck doubtfully, 'but beautiful you are not. Sure as eggs is eggs, there's only one word to describe you. Ugly!'

The Great Sloth Race

Dozy was a Two-fingered Tree-sloth.

On his feet he had three toes, but on each hand only two fingers.

Snoozy was a Three-fingered Tree-sloth. He also had three toes, but he had three fingers on each hand.

All tree-sloths spend their lives upside down in the forests of South America. They are born upside down, they live upside down, and the only time they ever touch the ground is when they die (upside down) and fall off their perches.

Always they are facing the sky, so that they see only the

tops of the trees, and when it rains, only their tummies get wet.

Dozy and Snoozy were quite different, and not just because Snoozy had more fingers.

Dozy was grumpy. He had a bad-tempered expression. He would bite, and slash with his sharp claws.

Snoozy was gentle. On his face he wore what looked like a smile. He only waved his arms about, and never bit anyone.

Dozy was brownish.

Snoozy was silvery.

Dozy was boastful.

Snoozy was modest.

Where they were alike was in the way they moved, and not just because it was upside down. It was also very, very slow.

All tree-sloths are slow, but Dozy and Snoozy were among the slowest sloths in the whole of South America.

Snoozy didn't mind this.

'Nice and easy does it,' he would say gently to himself as,

very, very slowly, he reached out with
one three-fingered hand to pull
himself forward.

Dozy did mind.

'Get a move on,' he would
say grumpily to himself
as, very, very slowly, he
reached out and pulled
himself forward with one
two-fingered hand.

The other creatures of the forest
made fun of Dozy and Snoozy. The
brightly coloured macaws screeched with laughter at the
tree-sloths, and the monkeys hung by their tails right in
front of the noses of Dozy and Snoozy and shouted, 'Slow
coach!' at them. Dozy slashed at them angrily, but Snoozy
only waved his arms about, while on his face he wore what
looked like a smile.

One day by chance Dozy and Snoozy met.

Snoozy was hanging under a branch having a nap when
Dozy came crawling along (upside down of course and

very, very slowly) underneath the same branch.

'Hey you!' said Dozy loudly. 'Get out of my way.'

Snoozy woke up.

'Oh, sorry,' he said softly, and he began to reverse. Now a sloth going backwards moves very, very, very slowly indeed, and while Dozy was waiting, he noticed Snoozy's hands.

He's got three fingers on each, he thought. Stuck-up creature. Snoozy noticed that Dozy had only two fingers on each hand. Poor chap, he thought.

'I suppose you think you're better than me?' said Dozy.

'Better?' said Snoozy. 'How do you mean?'

'I suppose you think you're faster than me, because you've got extra fingers?'

'Oh no,' said Snoozy. 'I shouldn't think so.'

'We'll see,' said Dozy. 'I challenge you to a race.'

By now Snoozy had reversed far enough to reach another nearby branch and thus get out of Dozy's way. He didn't want to race anyone, least of all this bad-tempered sloth.

But the monkeys had been listening, and they told the macaws, and the macaws flew all round the forest spreading the news.

'The Great Sloth Race!' they screeched. 'Roll up, roll up, everybody, to see the Great Sloth Race!'

There was no way now, it seemed to Snoozy, that he could escape having to race Dozy.

It took a long time of course before all was ready, but at last Dozy and Snoozy were hanging upside down on two long branches that ran parallel to one another.

Then the judge, an old and wise toucan, opened his enormous beak and called, 'Ready, steady, go!'

Very, very slowly, one with a two-fingered hand, one with a three-fingered, Dozy and Snoozy reached out to pull themselves forward. After an hour they had travelled about halfway along their branches. Dozy was slightly ahead.

Many of the animals of the forest who were watching had become bored and had flown or run or crawled or hopped away. After two hours, Dozy was well ahead and nearing the end of his branch.

By now everyone had become fed up with so slow a race, and all had gone away except the judge.

After three hours Dozy reached the end of his branch.

Opening his enormous beak, the toucan called, 'Stop! The race is over.'

Snoozy stopped.

'Told you so!' shouted Dozy. 'I got to the end first. I was faster than him, even though I've only got two toes on each hand and he's got three. I've won the race!'

The old wise toucan flew down and landed beside Snoozy.

'Oh dear,' he said softly. 'I should have explained the rules to Dozy. I'm afraid he went too fast. The object of a sloth race is to see who can go the slower. Congratulations, Snoozy. You are the winner.'

Upside down as always, Snoozy looked up at the toucan. On his face he wore what looked like a smile.

Blessu

Blessu was a very small elephant when he sneezed for the first time.

The herd was moving slowly through the tall elephant-grass, so tall that it hid the legs of his mother and his aunties, and reached halfway up the bodies of his bigger brothers and sisters.

But you couldn't see Blessu at all.

Down below, where he was walking, the air was thick with pollen from the flowering elephant-grasses, and suddenly Blessu felt a strange tickly feeling at the base of his very small trunk.

Hogsel
and
Gruntel

O nce upon a time there were two little piglets, brother and sister, called Hogsel and Gruntel. They were very unhappy, for their mother had died and their stepsow was not kind to them, so they ran away, into the forest.

They walked and walked, trotter in trotter, until they were exhausted and it seemed that they must die from hunger.

But suddenly they came upon a little house all made of gingerbread, with windows of transparent sugar.

'Saved!' cried Hogsel, and he tore off a piece of the roof and stuffed it in his mouth, while Gruntel helped herself to a window pane.

Just then an ancient crone appeared from inside the little house.

'Come in, little pigs!' she cried. 'You are hungry, I can see, so I will heat up the oven.' (And stick you both in it, she thought – nothing nicer than roast pork!)

So Hogsel and Gruntel went inside, and the old crone heated up the oven.

'See if it's hot enough,' she said. (And then I'll push you both in, she thought.)

'We're not tall enough to see into the oven,' said Hogsel, and, 'You have a look,' said Gruntel, and when the old crone did, they pushed her in and shut the oven door.

While she was cooking, Hogsel and Gruntel polished off

all the rest of the little gingerbread house and its sugar windows too. All that was left standing was the oven, from which came a strong smell of cooking crone.

'I'm full,' said Gruntel at last.

'Me too,' said Hogsel.

'What about her?' said Gruntel.

'I couldn't eat another thing,' said Hogsel.

So they left her to stew in her own juice.

The
Septopus

From the moment he was born, Conrad believed himself to be an octopus. His mother was an octopus, his father was an octopus, all his many brothers and sisters were octopuses.

Conrad had no idea that he was different.

Until the day of the Passing-out Parade.

Conrad's father was a rather strict octopus, and before his children left home to go and seek their fortunes in the great wide ocean, he always inspected them.

He lined them up, girls on the right, boys on the left.

His real name was Norton, but he was more often known as Norty.

Now some mother animals can wallop their young ones if they do not do what they are told. A lioness can cuff her cub, a monkey can clip its child round the ear, or an elephant can give her baby a biff with her trunk. But it's not so easy for hedgehogs.

'Sometimes,' said Hylda to Herbert, 'I wish that hedgepigs didn't have prickles.'

'Why is that, my dear?' said Herbert.

'Because then I could give our Norty a good hiding. He deserves it.'

'Why is that, my dear?' said Herbert.

'Not only is he disobedient, he has taken to answering me back. Why can't he be good like the others? Never have I known such a hedgepiglet. I shall be glad when November comes.'

'Why is that, my dear?' said Herbert.

Hylda sighed. Conversation with my husband, she said to herself for the umpteenth time, can hardly be called interesting.

'Because then it's time to hibernate, of course, and we can all have a good sleep. For five blissful months I shall not have to listen to that impudent, squeaky little voice arguing, complaining, refusing to do what I say and generally giving me cheek.'

Hylda should have known it would not be that easy.

When November came, she said to her husband and the seven children, 'Come along, all of you.'

'Yes, Mummy,' said the three good boys and the three

good girls, and, 'Why is that, my dear?' said Herbert, but Norty only said, 'Shan't.'

'Norty,' said Hylda. 'If you do not do what you are told, I shall get your father to give you a good hard smack.'

Norty fluffed up his spines and sniggered.

'You'll be sorry if you do, Dad,' he said.

'Where are we going, Mummy?' asked one of the hedgepiglets.

'We are going to find a nice deep bed of dry leaves, where we can hibernate.'

'What does "hibernate" mean, Mummy?' asked another.

'It means to go to sleep, all through the winter. When it's rainy and blowy and frosty and snowy outside, we shall all be fast asleep under the leaf pile, all cosy and warm. Won't that be lovely?'

'No,' said Norty.

'Norton!' said his mother angrily. 'Are you coming or are you not?'

'No,' said Norty.

'Oh well, stay here then,' snapped Hylda, 'and freeze to death!' and she trotted off with the rest.

In a far corner of the garden they found a nice deep bed of dry leaves, and Hylda and Herbert and the six good hedgepiglets burrowed their way into it, and curled up tight, and shut their eyes, and went to sleep.

The following April they woke up, and opened their eyes, and uncurled, and burrowed out into the spring sunshine.

'Goodbye, Mummy. Goodbye, Daddy,' chorused the six good hedgepiglets, and off they trotted to seek their fortunes.

'Oh, Herbert,' said Hylda. 'I feel so sad.'

'Why is that, my dear?' said Herbert.

'I should never have left our

Norty out in the cold last November. He will have frozen to death, poor little fellow. What does it matter that he was rude and disobedient and cheeky? Oh, if only I could hear his squeaky voice again, I'd be the happiest hedgepig ever!'

At that moment there was a rustling from the other side of the bed of leaves, and out came Norty.

'Can't you keep your voices down?' he said, yawning. 'A fellow can't get a wink of sleep.'

'Norty!' cried Hylda. 'You did hibernate, after all!'

'Course I did,' said Norty. 'What did you expect me to do – freeze to death?'

'Oh, my Norty boy!' said Hylda. 'Are you all right?'

'I was,' said Norty, 'till you woke me, nattering on as usual.'

'Now, now,' said Hylda, controlling herself with difficulty, 'that's not the way to speak to your mother, is it? Come here and give me a kiss.'

'Don't want to,' said Norty.

'Anyone would think,' said Hylda, 'that you weren't pleased to see us.'

'Anyone,' said Norty, 'would be right.'

'Well, push off then!' shouted Hylda. 'Your brothers and sisters have all gone, so get lost!'

'Shan't,' said Norty.

He yawned again, full in his mother's face.

'I'm going back to bed,' he said. 'So there.'

At this Hylda completely lost her temper.

'I've had enough!' she screamed. 'You're the rudest hedgepig in the world and your father's the most boring,

113

and I never want to see either of you again!' and she ran away as fast as she could go.

Herbert and Norty stared after her.

Norty scratched his fleas and sniffed very noisily.

'Looks like she's done a bunk, Dad,' he said.

'Yes,' said Herbert. 'Why is that, my dear?'

'Can't think,' said Norty. 'But then she always was prickly.'

The Princess and the Pig

A beautiful princess was one day walking along a country road when she saw a large pig sitting on the grass verge.

Being of a kindly nature, she stopped to speak to it.

'Hello, piggy,' she said with a smile.

'Hi,' said the pig. 'Though actually I'm a handsome youth. I upset the local witch, with the results you can see.'

'What did you say to her?' asked the princess.

'I called her a dirty smelly ugly evil old bag,' said the pig. 'So she put a spell on me. "Only a kiss from a beautiful

115

princess can change things now," she said, and off she went, cackling with laughter.'

'Oh,' said the princess.

She looked at the pig doubtfully.

But then, because she was of a kindly nature, she bent down and, shutting her eyes and screwing up her courage, planted a kiss on the end of the pig's rubbery snout.

Immediately the princess also turned into a pig.

Zap!

Of all the chameleons in Africa, Kenneth was the most unhappy. He couldn't change colour.

Kenneth could do all the other clever things that chameleons do.

He could walk along a thin branch, holding it with two fingers of each hand.

He could roll his eyes in different directions at the same time.

He could shoot out his long sticky tongue and, sometimes, zap a fly.

But his brothers and his sisters and his friends could do

the cleverest thing of all.

They could change the colour of their skins.

If they sat on a greenish leaf, they turned greenish.

If they sat on a reddish flower, they turned reddish.

If they sat on yellowish sand, they turned yellowish.

But Kenneth always stayed the same colour — a sort of muddy brown.

However hard he tried, he didn't seem to be able to get the hang of changing. He was always muddy brown.

So he could only zap flies when he sat on brown mud.

So he didn't zap many flies.

He was the most unhappy chameleon in Africa.

One day Kenneth was sitting on a leaf, trying to zap flies. The leaf was silvery, so the flies could see him easily; and one after another they buzzed off laughing.

'Oh dear!' said Kenneth, rolling his tongue back up, after the fifteenth miss.

'What's the trouble?' said a voice, and Kenneth looked round.

There on the next branch was a pretty young female chameleon whose name was Kiki.

Kenneth sighed.

'I'm feeling blue,' he said.

'You don't look it,' said Kiki. 'Why do you stay muddy brown on a silvery leaf?'

Kenneth was ashamed. He rolled his eyes in different directions.

'I can't change,' he said. 'All my brothers and sisters and friends can change colour, but I can't get the hang of it. I wish I could. I'm green with envy.'

'You don't look it,' said Kiki again. 'But,' she said softly, 'I'll tell you what you do look.'

'What?'

'You look very handsome.'

Kenneth felt terribly embarrassed.

'There!' she cried. 'You can do it!'

Kenneth kept one eye on Kiki, and rolled the other one backwards to look at himself. He had turned bright red!

'You see,' said Kiki, 'you felt embarrassed, didn't you?'

'Yes,' said Kenneth.

'Well, there you are. If you want to be green, for instance, try FEELING envious.'

So he tried, and sure enough, he turned green.

Then Kiki told him to pretend to feel frightened, and he turned yellow; and to feel angry, and he turned black; and to feel old and tired, and he turned grey.

'Now,' said Kiki, 'try feeling unhappy.'

'No,' said Kenneth, rolling his eyes madly. 'Now I've met you, blue's the one colour I'm never going to be. Let's go fly-zapping!'

And from then on, the flies never had another chance to laugh at Kenneth the chameleon.

ZAP! they never knew what hit them.